SERVICE FRANÇAIS DE LA BBC

JE SUIS, TU ES,

LA PLUME DE MA TANTE, LESSON NUMBER THREE

UN, DEUX, TROIS,

LA PLUME DE MA TANTE, LESSON NUMBER SIX
I COULD TELL YOU WHAT TO DO WITH THE PLUME OF YOUR BLOOMING TANTE, MATE

ICI PARIS

TRÈS BON!
WET PAINT
Keep off cat
PLANS
SOCKS, VESTS PANTS, SHIRTS, TROUSERS, JACKET, HATS....
TEA, SUGAR, CORNFLAKES, MARGE, KETCHUP, JAM, BAKED BEANS....
FLIPPER FEET, CAMERA, EASEL, TORCH BINOCULARS, BIRD BOOK

NORTHERN KENNELS INC

GOODBYE CAT

GOODBYE DOG

LA BELLE FRANCE!

-ER, BONJOUR, MADEMOISELLE
MADAME! S'IL VOUS PLAIT! BONJOUR, M'SIEUR

OH-ER, PARDON, **MADAME**-ER- JE VEUX ACHETER LE LAIT, S'IL VOUS PLAIT

DU LAIT? OUI, M'SIEUR

MERCI, MADAME!
MERCI, M'SIEUR!

I SPOKE FRENCH! I SPOKE FRENCH!

THIS IS THE LIFE!

WHAT'S THAT?

BLOOMING MARVELLOUS!

GOLDEN ORIOLE! NEVER SEEN ONE BEFORE. ONE MORE TO TICK OFF

BETTER GO SHOPPING IN A MINUTE

BLOOMING FUNNY BREAD

WISH I DIDN'T LOOK SO LIKE A BLOOMING FOREIGNER

AH!

BLEU DE TRAVAI
MAGNIFIQUE, M' SIEUR!

THAT'S BETTER- LOOK MORE FRENCH, NOW

NOT SO CONSPICUOUS

THAT AFTERNOON
BLOOMING MARVELLOUS LIGHT!

OH DEAR! FEEL A BIT QUEER IN THE TUM

OH DEAR!

WHERE'S THE ALKA-WHATSIT?

WHERE'S THAT DIO-STUFF?

OOOH, DEAR!

BLOOMING FLIES!

LIGHT A FIRE - THAT WILL FIX 'EM

OH, FOR A CHIMNEY!

OH DEAR, MY TUM!
BAP 748K
LA-THE CAFE
THAT NIGHT
NEXT MORNING
CRUMBS! WHAT A NIGHT! NOW THE WHOLE VAN IS ROCKING!
I FEEL SEA-SICK. BETTER GO FOR A WALK
SHOO! SHOO!
BETTER GET TO A PROPER CAMPING GROUND – TOILETS AND EVERYTHING

REGARD, MAMAN! C'EST PÈRE NOËL!
OH, VIENS VITE!
TIME TO BE MOVING ON
RES

OH CRUMBS! THAT'S DONE IT!

THAT EVENING
HERE, YOU KNOW THAT BLOKE WHO LOOKS LIKE FATHER CHRISTMAS?
YES, WHAT ABOUT HIM?

HE'S GOT TWO REINDEER WITH HIM
OH, GET AWAY!
DEFINITELY TIME TO BE MOVING ON

MUST GET OUT OF HERE
GUIDE to the WORLD

FIND SOMEWHERE MORE HYGIENIC- BETTER DRAINS
ATLA

NO DIARRHOEA- PURER WATER
GUIDE
MAP

PURE WATER.... **SCOTLAND!** OF COURSE!

THE BEST WATER IN THE WORLD! AFTER ALL THEY MAKE WHISKY WITH IT!

THE FOLLOWING EVENING
NEROS PALACE
HM, NOT BAD LITTLE HOTEL

NEROS
PALACE
THE GLORY OF NOW
LAS VEGAS
NEVADA